A BOOK ABOUT
GOD

by FLORENCE MARY FITCH

illustrated by

HENRI SORENSEN

Lothrop, Lee & Shepard Books * Morrow

New York

Everyone wonders about God . . .
Sometimes on a sunny afternoon
We look up at the blue sky.
Sometimes on a winter night,
When the stars are big and bright,
We think about Him
And wish we could see Him.
But we don't need to see God
to know what He is like.
We only need to think about the
things that are like Him.

The sky is like God . . .
Bright by day with the light
of the sun,
Restful and friendly at night
with moon and stars.

The sun is like God . . .
It is always shining.
Flowers turn their faces
toward the sun.
Trees stretch out their branches
to reach the sunshine

And spread their leaves till
every one receives the light.
The sun draws each growing thing
unto itself
And gives it life and strength.

Even on cloudy days
    we see the sun's light
    and feel its warmth.
Even at night, when we cannot
    see the sun,
The moon reflects some
    of its light.

The air is like God . . .
Air is all around us.
Even though we do not see it
we feel its warmth
and its coolness.
Without air outside us and
within us we cannot live.
Without God we cannot live.

The rain is like God's love—
    falling gently upon the earth,
    filling rivers and streams
    and springs.
We do not see the rain feeding
    the roots of plants and
    helping the seeds to sprout.
But we see the grass grow,
    the flowers blossom,
    and the fruits ripen.

We see God's life
in every growing thing.
In trees all beautiful
with little leaves in spring,
Deep and green with the cool
dark shade of summer,

Burning bright
    with colors of fall,
        in winter loveliest of all.

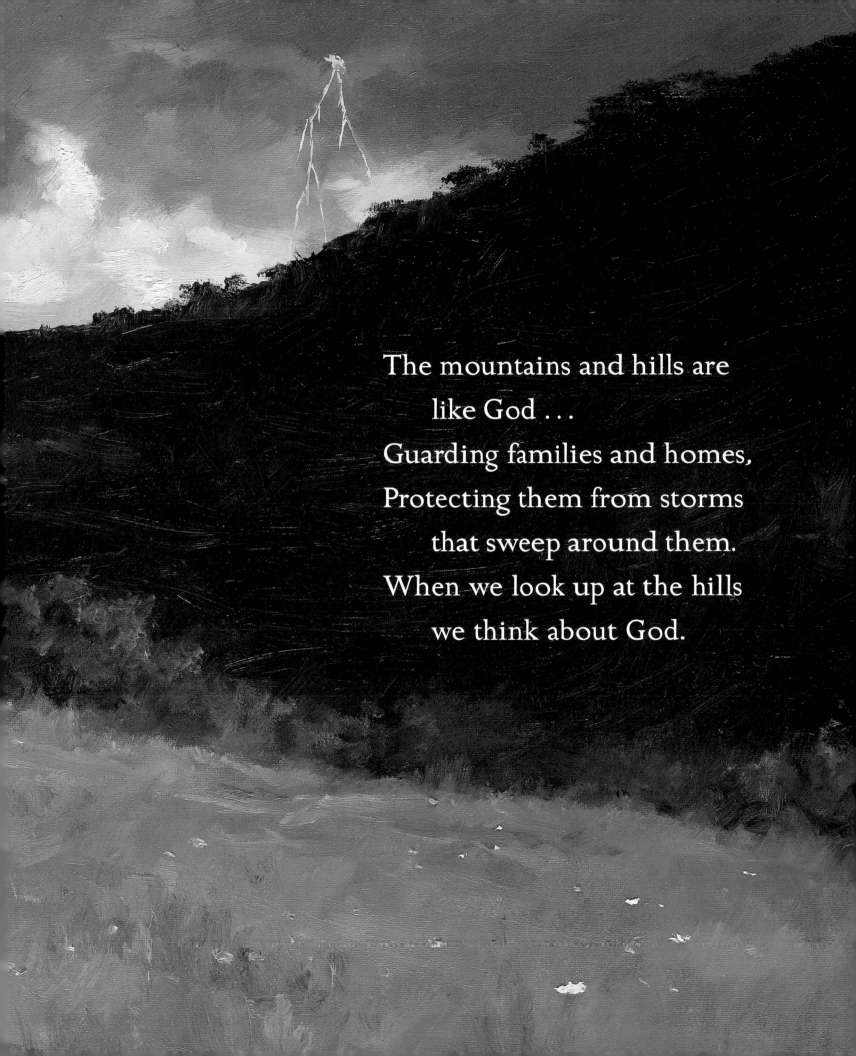

The mountains and hills are
like God . . .
Guarding families and homes,
Protecting them from storms
that sweep around them.
When we look up at the hills
we think about God.

And we remember the sea . . .
The sea that stretches on and on
 far beyond our sight,
The sea that on the surface
 moves as it will
But deep down is quiet and still
 and full of mystery.
God is like the sea.

All things beautiful
    are like God.
God is like all these
    and more . . .
No one can count
    the stars in the sky.
No one can count
    the ways God shows
    His love.

Oil paints were used for the full-color illustrations.
The text type is 22-point Golden Cockerell.

Published by Lothrop, Lee & Shepard Books
an imprint of Morrow Junior Books
a division of William Morrow and Company, Inc.
1350 Avenue of the Americas, New York, NY 10019
www.williammorrow.com

Printed in Singapore at Tien Wah Press.

10 9 8 7 6 5 4 3 2 1

Library of Congress Cataloging-in-Publication Data
Fitch, Florence Mary, 1875–1959.
A book about God / by Florence Mary Fitch; illustrated by Henri Sorensen.
p. cm.
Originally published: New York: Lothrop, Lee and Shepard, c1953.
Summary: Discusses God and how he is reflected in the natural world around us.
ISBN 0-688-16128-6 (trade)—ISBN 0-688-16129-4 (library)
1. God—Juvenile literature. [1. God. 2. Nature—Religious aspects.] I. Sorensen, Henri, ill.
II. Title. BT107.F5 1998 231—dc21 97-48682 CIP AC